"안녕하세요~"
말을 걸어오면 딸꾹

"Hello~"
When he starts talking to her – Hiccup!

"뭐 드릴까요?"
손이 스치면 딸꾹

"How can I help you?"
When the hands touch – Hiccup!

"여기 보세요."
눈이 마주치면 딸꾹

"Look here."
When their eyes meet – Hiccup!

딸꾹 딸꾹 딸꾹 딸꾹 딸꾹

Hiccup! Hiccup! Hiccup! Hiccup! Hiccup!

휴~ 살았다.

Phew~ Now I'm safe.

다녀왔어요, 엄마.

사람들을 만나면 자꾸만 딸꾹질이 나요.
그래서 난 엄마랑 있는 게 편해요.
어차피 아무도 나를 모를 테니깐.

I'm back, mommie.

I keep getting hiccups when I meet people.
So I like staying at home with you mom.
No one will know me anyway.

외롭지 않아.
그리고 내가 없으면 엄마가 외롭잖아.
그렇지?

I'm not lonely.
And if I'm not here, you'll be lonely.
Right, mom?

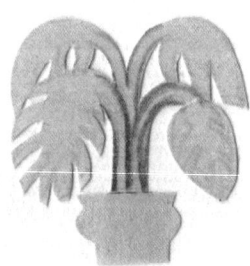

마을이 궁금하면 언제든지 볼 수 있어.

I can see the village whenever I feel curious.

오늘은 또 무슨 일이 일어날까?

I wonder what will happen today?

어? 어디로 가는 거지?

Oh? Where are they going?

다들 모여서 뭘 하는 거지?

What are they doing all together?

엄마, 모두 즐거워 보여요.

Mom, they look like they are having fun.

흥
나도 즐거워.
엄마도 즐겁지?

Huh!
I'm having fun too.
Mom is having fun too, right?

똑똑똑.

누구지?!

Knock - knock

Who is it?!

딸꾹

Hiccup!

엄마, 손님이 왔어.
딸꾹.

Mom, we have a guest.
Hiccup!

이름이 뭐야?
모른다고?

흠, 흠, 그럼. 내 소개부터 할까.
내가 누구인지 비밀이야.
너만 알고 있어야 해!
내 이름은 한나.

What's your name?
You don't know?

Hum, hum, alright! Then I'll introduce myself first.
It's a secret who I am.
You have to keep it a secret!
My name is Hanna.

우리 엄마, 예쁘지?

This is my mom. Pretty, isn't she?

사실 난 까만색보다 노란색을 좋아해.
꽃잎 같은 분홍색도 좋지, 하늘을 닮은 파란색은 또 어떻구!

I like yellow more than black.
Pink like petals, and blue like the sky!

나는 트럼펫을 즐겨 불어.
뽐뽐뿌 뿌뿌~

I like playing the trumpet.
Pom, pom pom, tararara, ra ra ra~

외발자전거 타기도 잘하지.
진짜 멋진 거 보여줄까?
외발자전거 타면서 트럼펫 불기!

I'm also good at riding a unicycle.
You want to see something really great?
I can play the trumpet while riding the unicycle!

뭐? 밖으로 나가자고?
안 돼!
왜 안 되냐고...?
나가면 딸꾹질이 멈추지 않고
딸꾹질이 멈추지 않고...
딸꾹질이 멈추지 않으니까!

안 돼! 거기 서!
밖으로 나가면 위험해!

What? Outside?
No!
Why not... ?
Because my hiccups won't stop if I go outside.
They won't stop...
They just carry on!

No! Stop!
It's dangerous outside!

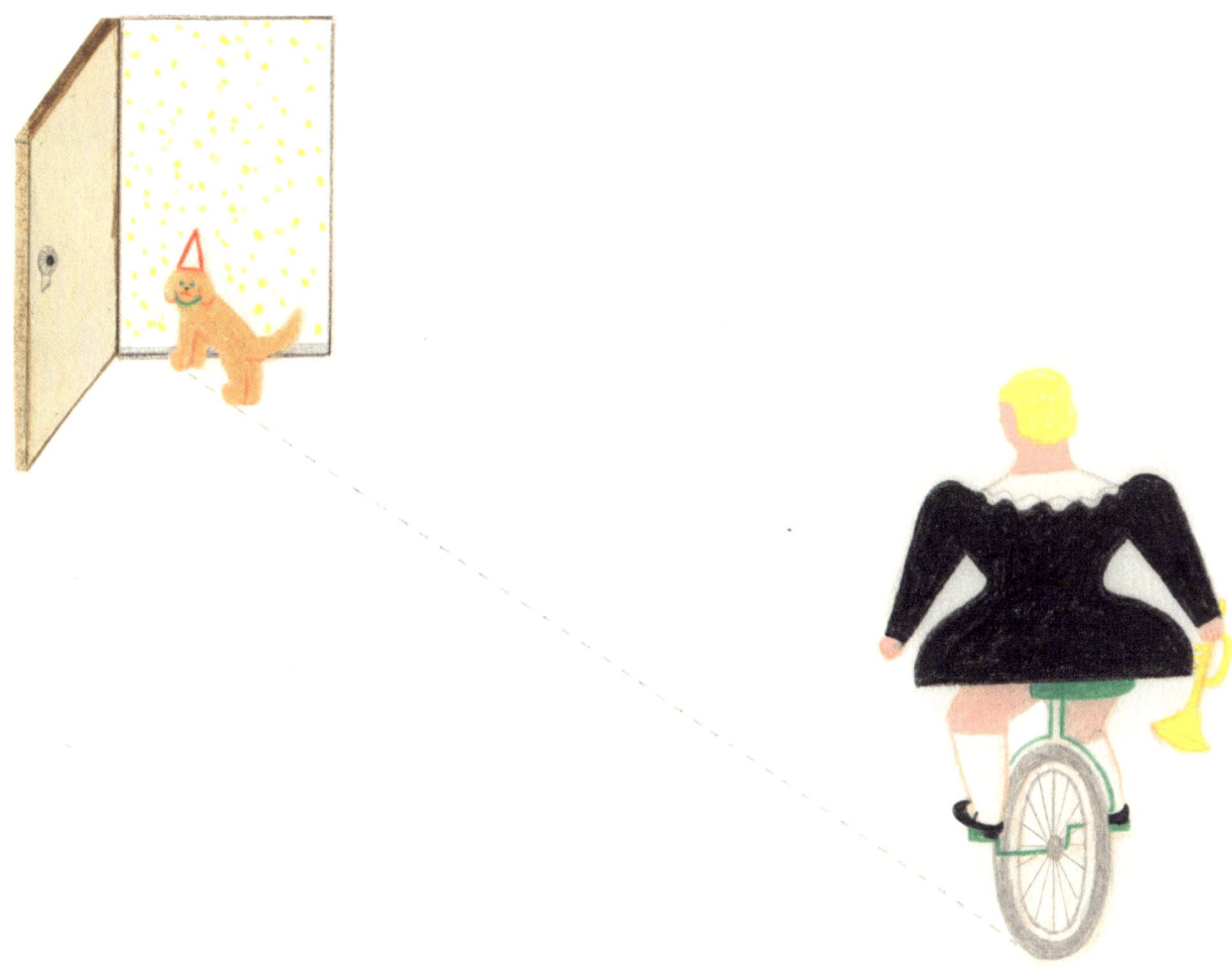

거기 서라고!
안 들리나? 에잇!
뿜뿜뿌 뿜뿌~!!!!

Stop right there!
Can't you hear me? Gosh!
Pom, pom pom, tararara, ra ra~!!!!

뿜뿜뿌 뿜뿌~!!!!

Pom, pom pom, tararara~!!!!

으악!!!

Ouch !!!

엄마, 난 이제 망했어요...

Mom, I'm doomed ...

"너 트럼펫을 정말 잘 부는구나."
딸꾹
"외발자전거를 이렇게 잘 타는 사람은 처음 봤어."
딸꾹
"니 이름이 뭐더라…"
딸꾹 딸꾹 딸꾹 딸꾹 딸꾹

"You play the trumpet very well."
Hiccup!
"I have never seen anyone who rides an unicycle so well."
Hiccup!
"What was your name…"
Hiccup! Hiccup! Hiccup! Hiccup! Hiccup!

아, 맞아!
넌 한나잖아. 한나.

우리 모두 너를 알아.

Well yes, that's true!
You're Hanna, right? Hanna?

We all know you.

어, 그거 비밀인데...
어떻게 알았지?

Oh, I thought that was a secret...
How did they know?

Epilogue